WELCOME TO
PASSPORT TO READING
A beginning reader's ticket to a brand-new world!

Every book in this program is designed to build read-along and read-alone skills, level by level, through engaging and enriching stories. As the reader turns each page, he or she will become more confident with new vocabulary, sight words, and comprehension.

These PASSPORT TO READING levels will help you choose the perfect book for every reader.

READING TOGETHER
Read short words in simple sentence structures together to begin a reader's journey.

READING OUT LOUD
Encourage developing readers to sound out words in more complex stories with simple vocabulary.

READING INDEPENDENTLY
Newly independent readers gain confidence reading more complex sentences with higher word counts.

READY TO READ MORE
Readers prepare for chapter books with fewer illustrations and longer paragraphs.

This book features sight words from the educator-supported Dolch Sight Words List. This encourages the reader to recognize commonly used vocabulary words, increasing reading speed and fluency.

For more information, please visit passporttoreadingbooks.com.

Enjoy the journey!

Little, Brown and Company
Hachette Book Group
1290 Avenue of the Americas, New York, NY 10104
Visit us at LBYR.com
enchantimals.com

First Edition: March 2019

Little, Brown and Company is a division of Hachette Book Group, Inc.
The Little, Brown name and logo are trademarks of Hachette Book Group, Inc.

The publisher is not responsible for websites (or their content) that are not owned by the publisher.

Library of Congress Control Number 2018953128

ISBN: 978-0-316-48737-5 (pbk.)

Printed in the United States of America

CW

10 9 8 7 6 5 4 3 2 1

Passport to Reading titles are leveled by independent reviewers applying the standards developed by Irene Fountas and Gay Su Pinnell in *Matching Books to Readers: Using Leveled Books in Guided Reading*, Heinemann, 1999.

Enchantimals™

SPRING
SCAVENGER HUNT

By Perdita Finn
Based on the episode "Peacock Puzzles"
by Keith Wagner

LITTLE, BROWN AND COMPANY
New York   Boston

Hello, Enchantimals friends!
Look for these words
when you read this book.
Can you spot them all?

blossom

berries

helmet

log

It is finally spring in Wonderwood.
Today is a special day.
Patter Peacock is making a
scavenger hunt for her friends.

Patter smiles.

She finished writing the last clue.

The scavenger hunt is ready!

Felicity Fox opens her door and finds a clue.

A paper airplane lands in Danessa Deer's antler.

A clue falls down
Bree Bunny's
chimney.

Sage Skunk sees a clue on her doorstep.

The girls and their besties are puzzled.
Felicity reads the first clue aloud.

The clue says, "Get ready
for something good:
an adventure through
Wonderwood!"

Then Bree reads her clue:
"You will solve clues along the way
to celebrate this special day."

"You need to follow your nose
to find something that grows!"
says Danessa's clue.

Sage's nose twitches.
She sniffs the paper.

Sage's bestie, Caper,
sniffs the paper, too.
It smells like a
Yearwood Blossom
flower!

Bree understands!
"We need to find a
Yearwood Blossom.
But those are hard to find."

Danessa and Sprint know
where to find one!

Along the way, the girls wonder
what makes this day so special.
"It is not time for the
Wonderwood Festival,"
says Danessa.

They finally find a
Yearwood Blossom!

The flower opens.
"That happens only once
a year," says Danessa.

The next clue is
inside the flower!

It says, "You will spy
some trees in the sky.
It is now or never,
you are berry clever."

Did someone say BERRIES?
Bree and her bestie, Twist,
know where ALL the berries are!
They can lead the way.

Flick finds the next clue
in the berry bushes!
"Great job, Flick," Felicity says.

"The next clue
offers a bird's-eye view,"
Felicity reads.

Is the clue at the top of a tree?
Maybe!

Twist eats some berries and puts
on a helmet to climb a tree.
She reaches the top and finds the clue!

The clue says,
"Meet us between Jungle and Wonder.
Get there quickly and do not blunder."

How will the girls travel?
Twist wipes the berry juice
with the clue and sees there
is more on the paper!

"Do you want a helping hand?
The best way to travel is not by land,"
the clue continues.

Sage thinks they should fly.
She flaps her arms, but none
of them have wings.

Felicity has another idea.
She leads her friends to
the Babbling Brook.

Sprint sees four logs.
They can ride the logs!

"Woo!" cry the girls and their besties.

Felicity remembers Patter and her bestie,
Flap, came to Wonderwood on a log.

The girls arrive at a special place.

"This is where we first met

Patter and Flap!" Bree says.

What a great surprise!
Patter and Flap are waiting
for their friends.
Patter has one more riddle.
"What is so special about this day?"

The girls think
about the clues:
a flower that blooms
once a year,

traveling on logs like
Patter and Flap,

and this special place.
Hmm...

"Today is the anniversary of Patter and Flap coming to Wonderwood!" shouts Felicity.

Flap spreads his tail feathers.

"That is right," Patter says.
"Every day with our friends
is an adventure.
So we gave YOU an
adventure today!"

Patter and Flap have
one more surprise.

A party!
Twist is so excited
that she jumps into
a bowl of berries!

Bree laughs.
"Go for it," she says.
"After all, today is a
BERRY special day."